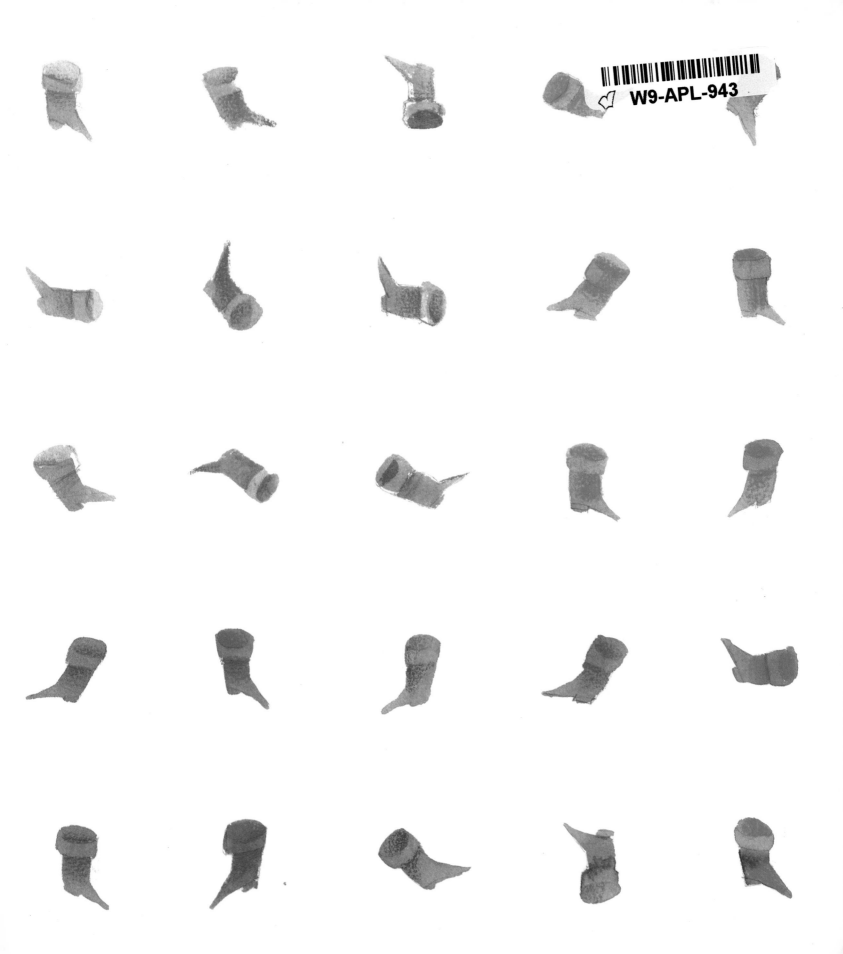

Left & Right

Text copyright © 1989 by Joanne Oppenheim
Illustrations copyright © 1989 by Rosanne Litzinger

Requests for permission to make copies of any
part of the work should be mailed to:
Copyrights and Permissions Department,
Harcourt Brace Jovanovich, Publishers,
Orlando, Florida 32887.

Library of Congress Cataloging-in-Publication Data
Oppenheim, Joanne.
Left & Right/by Joanne Oppenheim; illustrated by Rosanne
Litzinger. — 1st ed.
p. cm.
"Gulliver books."
Summary: Two quarreling cobbler brothers who specialize
in opposite feet learn it takes two to make a pair.
ISBN 0-15-200505-6
(1. Left and right—Fiction. 2. Shoemakers—Fiction. 3.Boots—
Fiction. 4. Brothers—Fiction. 5. Stories in rhyme.)
1. Litzinger, Rosanne, ill. II. Title. III. Title: Left and right.
PZ8.3.0615Le 1989
(E) — dc19   87-22939

Printed in Singapore
First edition
A B C D E

The illustrations in this book were done on
fine Italian handmade paper, using opaque
watercolors and colored pencils.
The text type was set in Barcelona
by Thompson Type, San Diego, California.
Printed and bound by Tien Wah Press, Singapore
Production supervision by Warren Wallerstein
and Eileen McGlone
Designed by Nancy J. Ponichtera

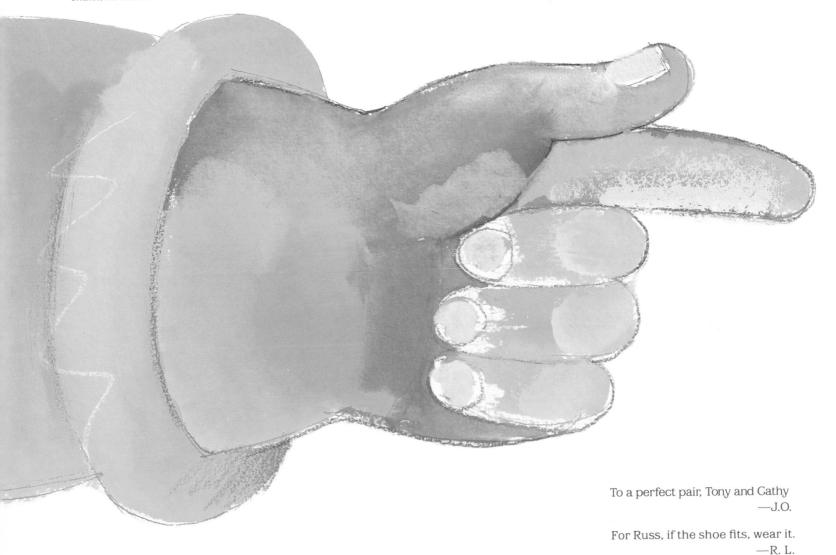

To a perfect pair, Tony and Cathy
—J.O.

For Russ, if the shoe fits, wear it.
—R. L.

Left & Right

WRITTEN BY
Joanne Oppenheim

ILLUSTRATED BY
Rosanne Litzinger

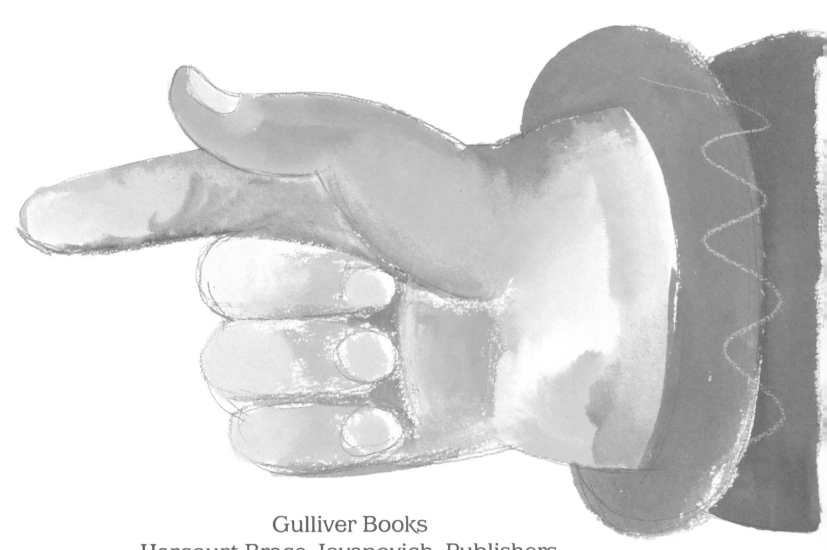

Gulliver Books
Harcourt Brace Jovanovich, Publishers
San Diego   New York   London

There once were two cobblers,
the cobblers were brothers.
These cobblers made boots
far better than others.

Left made the left boots.
Right made the rights.
They made many boots,
but they had lots of fights.

"That heel is too high."
"No, yours is too low."
"Don't hammer so fast."
"You hammer too slow."

"That boot is too dark."
"No, yours is too light."
"I say you are wrong."
"I say I am right."

Day after day
and night after night,

the two brother cobblers
had fight after fight.

Till one night Right said, "Left, I'm through!
I'm moving out—I don't need you!"

"Fine," Left said. "For once you're right!"
Then he booted Right out
and slammed the door tight!

The Mayor proclaimed, "It's all for the best.
Maybe, at last, we can all get some rest
with two cobbler shops . . .

. . . one east and one west."

On Monday the Farmer came into town
to order new boots of the darkest earth brown.

On Tuesday the Baker delivered fresh bread.
"I need some new boots. Make them white," he said.

So Left was happy. He had plenty to do.
Then the Mayor strolled in. He needed boots, too!

On Wednesday Right measured the Woodsman's feet,
and on Thursday morning he measured the Sweep.

But on Friday the Woodsman returned to the shop.
His right boot was fine, but the left made him hop.
And as for the Sweep, his boots were the same:
The right boot was fine, but the left gave him pain.

While over the river, the left boots all fit,
but the rights were wrong. They pinched quite a bit.

On Saturday the Woodsman hobbled to town.
"Come in," called the Doctor. "Come in and sit down."

And there were the Farmer, the Baker, the Sweep,
all sitting together and soaking their feet.

"Oh no," said the Doctor. "Not another, oh dear!
This soreness is catching. Catastrophic, I fear!
I must call the Mayor. This sickness may spread.
With trouble like this, we may all land in bed!"

He mentioned the Mayor, when who should arrive . . .
"Oh no!" said the Doctor. "Now there are five!"

"Do tell me," he said, as the five soaked their feet.
"When did this start . . . and what did you eat?"
The Mayor looked up, and so did the others.
"It's nothing we ate. It began with those brothers!"

They tried trading boots,
but they still were in pain.
They decided they'd just have
to go and complain.

First they knocked at Left's door and he shouted, "Come in!"
And weren't they surprised to see Right beside him.

Together they sat, as they had days ago.
Left said to the others, "We want you to know.
I'll make the left boots . . .
and he'll make the rights."

It takes two to make a pair . . . in spite of the fights.

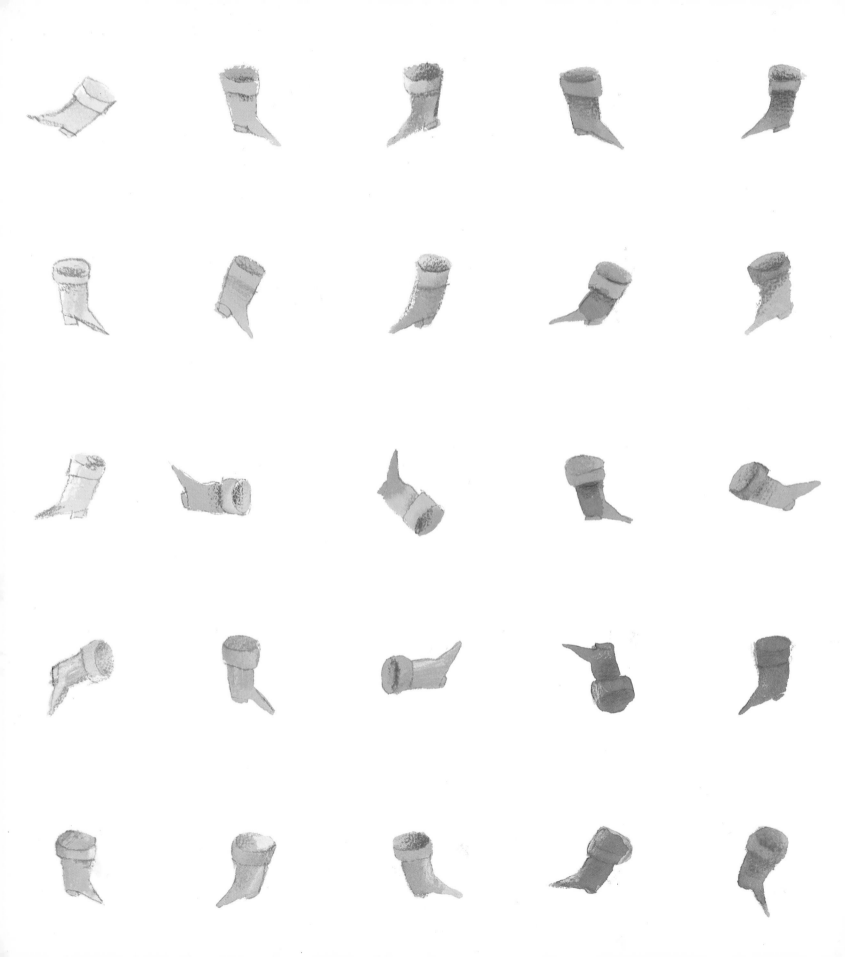